Riley Reynolds

SLAYS THE PLAY

created by

JAY ALBEE

STONE ARCH BOOKS
a capstone imprint

Published by Stone Arch Books, an imprint of Capstone
1710 Roe Crest Drive, North Mankato, Minnesota 56003
capstonepub.com

Library of Congress Cataloging-in-Publication Data is available
on the Library of Congress website
ISBN: 9781666344066 (hardcover)
ISBN: 9781666344103 (paperback)
ISBN: 9781666344141 (ebook PDF)

Summary: Nonbinary student Riley and their friends learn what
it takes to put on a school play.

Special thanks to Manu Shadow Velasco for their consultation.

Designed by Nathan Gassman

Printed and bound in the USA. 4882

TABLE OF CONTENTS

I'M RILEY!

I LOVE SO MANY THINGS! I LOVE CRAFTING.

THE ONLY THING BETTER THAN MAKING MESSES IS MAKING COOL STUFF.

I LOVE MY PARENTS, MY COUSINS, AND MY FRIENDS.

I LOVE DOGS AND CATS . . .

AND BIRDS AND FISH . . .

AND DRAGONS AND UNICORNS AND ALL ANIMALS!

I'M NONBINARY, AND I LOVE THAT TOO. I DON'T HAVE TO BE A BOY OR A GIRL.

I CAN JUST BE ME!

MX. AUDE TEACHES HELPFUL TERMS

Cisgender: Cisgender, or "cis" people, identify with the gender written on their birth certificate. They are usually boys or girls.

Gender identity: Regardless of the gender written on a person's birth certificate, they decide their gender identity. It might change over time. A person's interests, clothes, and behavior might be traditionally associated with their gender identity, or they might not.

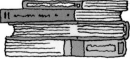

Honorific: Young people use honorifics when they talk to or about adults, especially teachers. Mr. is the honorific for a man, Mrs. or Ms. for a woman, and Mx. is the gender-neutral honorific often used for nonbinary people. It is pronounced "mix." Nonbinary people may also use Mr., Mrs., or Ms. as well.

LGBTQ+: This stands for lesbian, gay, bisexual (also pansexual), transgender, queer. There are lots of ways people describe their gender and attraction. These are just a few of those ways. The + sign means that there are many, many more, and they are all included in the acronym LGBTQ+.

Nonbinary: Nonbinary people have a gender identity other than boy or girl. They may be neither, both, a combination, or sometimes one and sometimes the other.

Pronouns: Pronouns are how people refer to themselves and others (she/her, they/them, he/him, etc.). Pronouns often line up with gender identity (especially for cis people), but not always. It's best to ask a person what pronouns they like to use.

Queer: An umbrella term for people who identify as LGBTQ+.

Transgender: Transgender (or trans) people do not identify with the gender listed on their birth certificate. They might identify as the other binary gender, both genders, or another gender identity.

CHAPTER ONE

ONE HOUR TO SHOWTIME

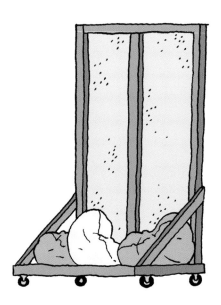

"Great rehearsal, fourth graders!" Mx. Aude yelled over the hubbub in the school auditorium.

Riley's fourth-grade class had just finished the dress rehearsal for the school premiere of their class play, *Dogs*. They had spent months writing the play together as a class. And now, *finally*, it was showtime!

Most of the class were in costume—a dalmatian, a Labrador, a spaniel, a poodle, a Great Dane, a greyhound—so many kinds of dogs! Not everyone was a specific breed of dog, but you could tell they were supposed to be a dog of *some* kind.

"Gather round!" Mx. Aude was the school librarian and the director of the play. Riley and their classmates stomped off the stage and gathered around Mx. Aude.

Mx. Aude looked at their clipboard. They flipped thoughtfully through the pages. "No notes!" they said. That meant there was no feedback.

"No notes?" asked Riley's class.

"None at all?" Riley said.

"That's right. You all did great!" said Mx. Aude, ready to move on to rehearsing the second-grade play.

"But it was a disaster!" said Georgie, who was playing the lead role of the bulldog. "Marco won't quit goofing around!"

"And I got paint all over my tail!" said Olivia.

Olivia was playing the golden retriever and had swept her big, fluffy tail over some wet paint on the backdrop.

"Oh no!" said Riley. "Olivia smudged the backdrop!"

Riley wasn't playing a dog. Instead, they had helped design the set and costumes. Riley and their dad had worked right up until the last moment on the backdrop, which was why the paint was still wet.

Lea and Cricket, Riley's best friends, whispered to each other. Lea, who was playing the Siberian husky, said, "I can't remember my line."

Cricket, playing the basset hound, replied, "I'm not even going to talk about how my ears keep falling off!"

Tunde, who was playing the corgi, overheard and said, "I missed my cue *again*."

"I still don't understand what a cue is!" Olivia said.

"It's how you know when it's time to say your line," Riley whispered to her.

Marco, playing the Pomeranian, said in a loud, silly voice, "I thought it was super-duper great!"

"See!" said Georgie. "Mx. Aude! Tell Marco he needs to take this seriously!"

Mx. Aude held their hand up high, which was their sign for quiet. The fourth graders simmered down. "Look, fourth grade, it's only an hour until curtain. I've got fifth graders having tantrums, second graders singing off-key, and third graders who can't remember their choreography. Trust me, your play could win awards."

Maddie, a fourth grader who hated dressing up, was Mx. Aude's assistant director. She nodded in agreement. "You really could win awards."

Mr. Lane, Riley's teacher, who had been there to cheer for the students, spoke up.

"Can we use the library for another practice run?" he asked Mx. Aude.

"Please," said Mx. Aude with relief.

"Come on, fourth graders!" said Mr. Lane. "To the library!"

"Wait, Mr. Lane," said Riley, "I have to find my dad and fix the backdrop."

"Sure, Riley. Come to the library when you're done."

"Okay," said Riley, dashing backstage.

CHAPTER TWO

RILEY'S BACKDROP

Backstage, Riley found Dad mounting

a backdrop. He was using a power drill to

screw painted panels onto wooden frames

that could be wheeled out onto the stage.

He was reusing the forest backdrop from

last year's high school play. It would be

the set for the fifth graders' play about camping and the third graders' play about fairies. The set for *Dogs* was painted over the backdrop from the winter break jukebox musical. What used to be a carousel scene was now a backyard with a doghouse (both of which Riley helped to paint). It doubled as the second grader's set too.

"Dad!" said Riley.

"Hey, Ry, how was rehearsal?" he asked.

"Mx. Aude said we could win an award, but Lea can't remember her line and Cricket's ears keep falling off and some kids messed up their cues. Georgie's not having fun, which is weird because

I thought he loved acting. And I just explained to Olivia what cue means."

"Slow down, Ry," said Dad, putting his drill back on his tool belt.

"And that's not even the worst part! Olivia's tail smudged the doghouse!"

"Huh, how about that," said Dad. "Show me."

Riley and Dad sneaked onto the stage behind the rehearsing second graders, including Riley's neighbor, Nelle.

"See?" said Riley, pointing out the doghouse.

"I see it."

Mx. Aude called out to Riley and Dad. "Everything okay up there?"

"It will be," replied Dad with a wave.

Mx. Aude gave a thumbs-up and turned back to the second graders.

Dad took Riley's hand. "Follow me."

Dad led Riley into the auditorium, where some parents were setting up chairs. There would be a big crowd to see the show—and the smudged doghouse.

Dad and Riley sat in the back row. Dad tipped his chin toward the stage.

"Look at Nelle," he said.

In the second grader play, a kid's toys all come to life. There were aliens and mermaids, superheroes and astronauts, a dinosaur, a robot, a stack of blocks, and Nelle, playing a helicopter. Riley gasped as Nelle transformed from plastic and still to animated and alive.

"Wow!" said Riley. "She's really good!"

"Right?" said Dad. "Now look at the doghouse."

Riley realized that while the backdrop set the scene, it was the actors who really drew the eye.

Riley looked harder at the backdrop. It was kind of magical how the green paint with bits of detail didn't really look like grass, but somehow made Riley think *exactly* of grass. And the darker lines on the doghouse made them think of wooden panels. Riley only saw the smudge because they knew where to look.

"Huh," said Riley. "How about that. It seemed way worse up close."

Mx. Aude called, "Mr. Reynolds? Is the forest set ready?"

"Ten minutes," Dad called. He turned to Riley with a wink. "Back to work."

As Riley and Dad walked back toward the stage, Riley watched the smudge. They could see it more clearly, but they could see other things too. They could see the tape on the astronaut costume, the alien's lopsided wig, and the seams between the backdrop's panels.

But none of it mattered compared to how the play made Riley *feel*. That was what really mattered.

Riley said, "I can see the smudge, but it doesn't make me think 'that's not even a real doghouse!' It almost makes the set better because it's not perfect. Like, it doesn't have to be perfect to still make me think *doghouse*."

Dad agreed. "I know! I love how a play makes an audience suspend their disbelief for a while."

"What does that mean?" asked Riley.

"Like, when we sit in the audience, we know for sure that this is a stage and not a yard. We know that that's our neighbor Nelle and not a helicopter toy come to life. But for a little while, it doesn't matter. We are happy to believe that these things are true. It helps us enjoy the play."

"I like that," said Riley. "I know that feeling, but I didn't know the words for it."

"It's one of the things that makes theater so special," Riley's dad said.

"It makes other things special too, like playing pretend a box is a car, or a couch is a castle, or a teddy is a doctor when we play hospitals. Hey! Is that why this is called a play?" Riley asked.

Dad laughed, "It might be! Makes sense to me." He gave Riley a quick squeeze.

Before Dad headed backstage to his forest, he said, "About Georgie. Sometimes I get a job I think will be fun, and it turns out to be hard work. I can forget what I was excited about in the first place. Maybe that's what's up with Georgie?"

"Maybe. Thanks, Dad," said Riley, and headed for the library to find out.

CHAPTER THREE

OLIVIA'S TAIL

In the library, the fourth graders had
pushed all the tables to the side to make
a space almost as big as the stage. Mr.
Lane held a copy of the script and was
coaching Tunde to hit his cues. He was

supposed to jump out of a bath, shout "Squirrel!" and zoom across the stage. He was sprinkled with silver glitter which went flying to look just like water. The joke wasn't funny unless he zoomed at just the right moment. Mr. Lane was doing his best, and so was Tunde. Olivia was trying to get Mr. Lane's attention.

"Mr. Lane!" said Olivia. "I have to fix my tail! It's got paint all over it!"

Mr. Lane said, "Does it wash out?"

"I tried that already," huffed Olivia. "It made it worse. Now it's got paint on it, *and* it's wet."

Olivia saw Riley and said, "Your backdrop messed up my tail!"

Olivia looked like she was about to cry. Riley was surprised. Olivia was usually cool, calm, and collected. She must have been really stressed about the tail.

"Please help me fix it!" she shouted.

Riley could see that Olivia was lashing out. But they knew it was because Olivia cared. Riley looked at the soggy, yellow-and-red tail. Riley wondered if this problem was the same as the problem of the doghouse.

"Go stand over there," said Riley, taking the tail and pointing to one end of the library. "Pretend you're in the audience and I'm you, onstage."

"Okay, I guess," said Olivia.

Riley walked to the other end of the library. Then Riley held up Olivia's tail and did a bit of the dance that Olivia performed in *Dogs*.

Riley had to make up a few steps because they couldn't remember them all. When Riley was done, they walked back to Olivia.

"Did you notice the paint?" asked Riley.

"Yeah, I did," said Olivia. She tilted her head a little. "But I was looking more at your dance moves."

"Right!" said Riley. "I think that's what the audience will notice too. And maybe they'll think you're a golden retriever with red fur in your tail."

Olivia thought about that for a moment. "Okay," she said, finally. "But it still looks weird that it's wet."

Riley agreed. "You can use the hand dryer in the bathroom. I did that to dry my hair last week when I got rained on."

"Great idea!" said Olivia, smiling wide. Her face fell. "I'm sorry I messed up your backdrop."

"Thanks, Olivia, but it's not actually too bad. Like the tail, I don't think the audience will notice too much. It'll be okay," Riley said.

"Good," said Olivia, no longer near tears. She took her tail and trotted to the bathroom.

Riley spotted Lea and Cricket, fiddling with the ears on Cricket's costume. Riley headed over to them just as Mr. Lane called out, "Thirty minutes until curtain!"

The library burst into nervous cheers and gasps and squeals. Riley included.

31

CHAPTER FOUR

CRICKET'S EARS

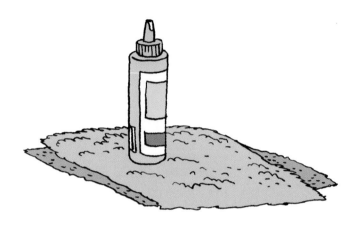

Riley, Lea, and Cricket all looked at Cricket's ears, which he held in his basset hound paws. "What if I glue them to my head?" He did the *beep-boop* noises he made when he was being a robot computer. "Beep-beep. Chance of regret, one hundred percent. Boop."

Lea said, "Maybe just don't wear them? Would that be better than them falling off right in the middle of the play?"

"Beep-boop. Cannot calculate," said Cricket.

"Your line is all about hearing things," said Riley. "That might sound weird coming from a dog with no ears."

"Oh, yeah," said Lea. "Good point."

Riley saw Cricket's sad face. Cricket was one of Riley's best friends. They hated to see him so down.

Riley smiled. "Cricket, remember that Halloween when you were a skeleton? You sat down weird and broke the butt bones on your costume? Who helped you fix that?"

"You did," said Cricket, smiling a bit.

"That's right, I did. And I'm going to help you fix these ears!"

"Chance of success, ninety-five percent, boop-beep!" said Cricket. "What should we do?"

"Can you show me again how they keep falling off?" asked Riley.

Cricket put his big, droopy, furry ears back on. He performed his line and the actions about hearing all kinds of noises in the neighborhood. When he swung his head around from side to side, listening for noises from all over, his ears fell off.

"I think they're too heavy," said Riley.

Riley had designed the costumes for each dog in the whole play. The ears were glued to headbands. The tails were tied around waists. The gloves were painted like paws. Riley had loved it, but it was a really big job.

And the way the class had interpreted Riley's designs was super fun to see. Everyone brought their own personality to the costume, just like each dog had their own personality.

Riley had made Cricket's ears for him. Riley used some lush brown velvet that they had been saving for a special occasion. They had glued on extra fur and sequins and padded the ears. Close up they really looked like soft, silky, droopy hound ears.

Cricket had felt extra special when Riley gave him the ears. They were the best ones in the whole play. Riley had worked really hard on them.

But now Riley and Cricket both knew that it didn't matter how good they looked, how hard Riley had worked, or how proud Cricket was—the ears just didn't work.

"Don't worry," said Riley. "I'll make you some more."

"Can I keep these?" asked Cricket.

"Sure!" said Riley.

Cricket beamed. "I'm going to wear them when I walk Mom's dog on the weekend!"

Riley, Lea, and Cricket gathered all the supplies Riley would need for the new ears—fabric, burlap, glue, and scissors— and put them in a big pile. Riley got right to work. Their friends helped whenever they could.

And in no time at all, the new ears were ready. Cricket put them on. He swung his head from side to side and the ears stayed on! He did it again, with even more swing, and they *still* stayed on.

The dark burlap wasn't as soft and silky as the velvet, but it swung and bounced in ways that the velvet hadn't. Cricket swung his head in all kinds of directions. He even spun around. Lea and Riley laughed. The new ears were funnier than the perfect ears had been, which made them better in their own way.

"Thanks, Riley," said Cricket. "These new ears are really fun!"

"That reminds me," said Riley, looking at Georgie, who wasn't having any fun at all.

CHAPTER FIVE

GEORGIE'S FUN

Riley went over to Georgie, who was standing in a corner of the library. He was yelling at Marco again.

Riley said, "Whoa, Georgie. Are you okay?"

"No!" shouted Georgie. "Marco won't stop goofing around."

Marco put his hands on his hips like Georgie and made a squished-up face.

Riley chuckled a little. "He got a bunch of laughs for being goofy in rehearsal. The audience will laugh too."

"But he's not taking it seriously!" said Georgie.

"Of course not. It's Marco. He doesn't take anything seriously."

Marco said, "Hey! Not true. I take being silly very seriously." He did a funny little dance. Riley laughed. Georgie fumed.

Riley looked at Georgie. "Maybe *you're* taking it a little *too* seriously?" Georgie blinked in surprise.

Riley went on, "I remember when you got the big part. You were so happy. You did a silly dance of your own then. You said it was going to be fun. But it doesn't seem like you're having fun at all now."

Georgie blinked again. Riley wasn't sure whether Georgie was mad or sad. Georgie sighed and smiled. Riley hadn't expected that!

"You are so right! I forgot that this is *supposed* to be fun. Oh, wow. How could I forget something so simple?" Georgie asked, shaking his head.

"It's easy to get carried away," Riley said.

"Marco, I'm sorry I yelled at you. You're really funny in the play. I guess I just haven't been in a funny mood. You should be as goofy as you want," Georgie said.

Marco couldn't really do a funny impression of Georgie when Georgie was being so sincere.

Georgie continued. "I was so ready to have fun as the bulldog. But instead I've been serious and snooty like my cat! But I'm a bulldog! And bulldogs are silly!"

"You're a great actor, Georgie. You can do it," said Riley.

"Maybe. Hmm." Georgie looked at Marco thoughtfully. He did the dance that Marco had done just before. Marco's version was bouncy and his arms flailed around. When Georgie did it, he was low to the ground and heavy, just like a bulldog.

Riley laughed. "You don't look like a cat *at all*."

Georgie laughed. "I can take being silly seriously too!"

Marco barked in approval and agreement.

"Perfect," said Riley. "And if you forget, look for me in the back of the audience. I was going to watch from backstage, but I'll make sure you can see me from the stage. When you see me, you'll remember."

Georgie hugged Riley tight.

45

CHAPTER SIX

LEA'S LINE

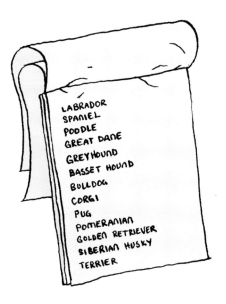

Riley, Marco, and Georgie laughed and laughed at Georgie's bulldog dance. Lea and Cricket came over. So did Olivia, tail super-fluffed up, and Tunde, who had finally nailed his cues.

Mr. Lane called out, "Okay, who's next?" and started to help another kid with something. Lea sighed.

"Do you need Mr. Lane?" Riley asked Lea.

"I'm not sure Mr. Lane can help," replied Lea. "I keep forgetting my line. I just can't do it. It's impossible."

"You got the hardest one in the whole play," agreed Cricket.

Lea's line was a list of all of the dog breeds that the fourth graders were dressed up as. When Lea called out a dog breed, the kid dressed as that dog would strike a pose. But Lea kept getting stuck. She kept forgetting what came after the pug. Riley could see that Lea was embarrassed.

"Let me hear it," said Riley.

Lea tried, she really did, but she just couldn't remember. Worrying about messing up made her keep messing up!

"Wait, what comes after pug?" asked Olivia.

"Me!" said Marco. "Pomeranian! Arf! Arf!" Everyone laughed at Marco, even Lea.

"That's it! Pomeranian! I think I'm getting stuck on–" Lea started.

"Arf! Arf!" interrupted Marco and everyone laughed.

"Pomeranian," Lea continued. "Because I run out of breath on pug."

Riley thought about other times Lea forgot to breathe, like when she was taking a penalty shot in a soccer match. She'd always missed, until she practiced how to take a step back, take a breath, and then take the shot. Now she netted nearly every shot!

Marco yipped again. "What if after pug, I say 'Pomeranian! Yip! Yip!' so you can take a breath?" he asked.

Marco was excited to have an extra line and another chance to get a laugh. Riley could see that, and it would help Lea to have a beat.

Riley watched Lea laughing at Marco's yip yipping. They could see how Lea's laugh reaction made her step out of her worry about messing up. It forced her to breathe and relax. You can't hold your breath and laugh at the same time. You just can't!

"I think that's a really good idea, Marco," said Riley.

"Me too," said Lea. "Let's try it."

The group ran through Lea's line. When Lea said "pug," she stopped and took a breath. She laughed at Marco, who said, "Pomeranian! Yip! Yip!"

Then, like magic, she kept going through the second half of the list. They ran it through one more time. Lea nailed it again!

"You got it!" Cricket whooped.

"I think this will work," Lea grinned.

Mr. Lane came over. "Sorry, Lea. There's been a lot going on. But I didn't forget about you. You wanted help remembering your line?"

"I think we've figured it out, Mr. Lane," Lea answered.

"Okay, great. Well done!" said Mr. Lane.

Which was lucky, because right then Riley's dad burst into the library and announced, "Five minutes till curtain!"

CHAPTER SEVEN

SHOWTIME!

Backstage was a flurry of activity. The fourth graders' play was first. An array of dogs stood on the stage, in front of their doghouse backdrop and behind the heavy red velvet curtain.

On the other side of the curtain, the auditorium filled up with friends and family.

Lea practiced breathing after pug. Cricket flipped and flopped his new ears back and forth. Georgie refined his bulldog butt-waggle dance. Olivia fluffed her tail. The only person perfectly still and at ease was Marco.

Riley checked in with Dad backstage.

"Everything ready?" Riley asked.

"Ready as it will ever be," he said with a wink.

Like Marco, Dad was at ease. Riley had seen Dad feel that way before. When a project was finished, he relaxed. Not always because the work was done, but sometimes because the deadline was up and there was nothing more he could do. Riley hugged Dad hard. And he hugged Riley back.

"We did great work together," Riley's dad said.

"We sure did! Come on," Riley said, tugging Dad across the curtained stage toward the steps to the auditorium.

As they passed each classmate, Riley said "Break a leg!" and so did Dad. It was a common phrase you said to actors that meant good luck. It was a long line of "Break a leg! Break a leg! Break a leg! Break a leg!" from one side of the stage to the other.

Riley said, "We'll be at the very back of the auditorium if you need to see a friendly face!"

In a moment, Riley and Dad were at the back of the room, next to a bunch of parents taking videos on their phones. They stood next to Nelle's dad, who gave a big thumbs-up. Mx. Aude came onto the stage and held up their hand for quiet.

Mx. Aude seemed calm like Dad, in that "it's-the-deadline-we-did-what-we-could" kind of way.

"Welcome, friends and family, to this year's play night!" The crowd hollered and cheered and whooped. And they hadn't even seen the show yet! "Our fourth-grade class is pleased to present a show they wrote together . . . *Dogs*." The audience clapped. Riley clapped the loudest of all.

The curtain slowly went up.

"Wow!" Riley said.

Their friends and classmates stood in their costumes under the lights, with the rest of the auditorium dark. Right then, Riley found it easy to suspend disbelief.

The set Riley and their dad had made looked amazing. The colors popped under the lights. Riley was so proud of their hard work. Especially the doghouse, smudge and all.

Before Georgie delivered the first line of the play, he looked out into the auditorium and found Riley. Riley gave a little wave and a thumbs-up. Georgie smiled. Riley knew he would take his silliness just seriously enough.

Some other kids looked for Riley too. Lea and Cricket beamed all the way to Riley in the back row. Riley smiled as bright as a spotlight.

Then Georgie took a deep breath . . . and the play began!

THE END

DISCUSSION QUESTIONS

1. To put on the class play, lots of people had different jobs to do. What kinds of jobs are there? What qualities or interests would make a person suited to each job?

2. What problems did Riley's class face between dress rehearsal and curtain? How did they solve those problems?

3. Georgie had trouble remembering to have fun. What kinds of things can get in the way of something being fun?

WRITING PROMPTS

1. Pretend you are a reporter and write a review of *Dogs* for your school newspaper. Did you enjoy the class play? What did you think about the sets, the costumes, the actors, and the script?

2. If you were in a play, what part would you want? Would you want to be backstage or onstage performing? Write a few paragraphs explaining your answer.

3. Riley and their class had to do some quick thinking and problem solving. Write about a time you solved a problem in an unusual or unexpected way.

MEET THE CREATORS

Jay Albee is the joint pen-name for LGBTQ+ couple Jen Breach and J. Anthony. Between them they've done lots of jobs: archaeologist, illustrator, ticket taker, and bagel baker, but now they write and draw all day long in their row house in South Philadelphia, PA.

Jen has never been in a play. J. is the stage star of this partnership.

Jen Breach

J. Anthony